For the Old Guru, Brian

First published in Great Britain in 1998 by Ragged Bears Limited,
Ragged Appleshaw, Andover, Hampshire SP11 9HX

Text and illustration copyright © 1998 by Jacqueline East

The right of Jacqueline East to be identified as the author and illustrator
of this work has been asserted

A CIP record of this book
is available from the British Library

ISBN 1 85714 144 X

Printed in Hong Kong

I Can't...

Jacqueline East

Ragged Bears

"Ow!" yelled Ed.

"I can't climb trees!" groaned Ed.

"Then sit quietly and do some painting,"
suggested his mum.

"I can't paint!" Ed grumbled.

"Well, would you like to help me in the kitchen?" asked Ed's mum.

"I can't cook!" wailed Ed.

"You must never say 'can't' Edward," said mum.

Just then Elsie ran past the window with
Ed's favourite toy!

"You come back, right now Elsie!"
shouted Ed and he chased her right to the
top of a tree.

Before he realised he had climbed a tree, there was a CRACK and they both fell in the water.

"Help, I can't swim!" gasped Elsie.

"Never say 'can't' Elsie," said Ed

and he taught her to swim.

They rushed home hand in hand.

"I can climb trees!" shouted Ed.
"And I can swim!" shrieked Elsie.

"And I can see two very muddy animals!"
said mum.

She gave them some biscuits and warm
towels and Edward tried hard never to say
'I can't' again!